WALT DISNEY'S
SNOW WHITE
And The Seven Dwarfs

A GOLDEN BOOK • NEW YORK

Western Publishing Company, Inc., Racine, Wisconsin 53404

© 1984 The Walt Disney Company. "Heigh-Ho" © 1938 Bourne Co. Copyright renewed. Words by Larry Morey, Music by Frank Churchill. Used by permission. All rights reserved. Printed in the U.S.A. No part of this book may be reproduced or copied in any form without written permission from the copyright owner. GOLDEN®, GOLDEN & DESIGN®, and A GOLDEN BOOK® are trademarks of Western Publishing Company, Inc. Library of Congress Catalog Card Number: 85-51645. ISBN 0-307-10205-X/ISBN 0-307-60305-9 (lib. bdg.)
C D E F G H I J

Long ago, in a faraway kingdom, there lived a lovely young Princess named Snow White.

Her stepmother, the Queen, was cruel and vain. She hated anyone whose beauty rivaled her own—and she watched her stepdaughter with angry, jealous eyes.

The Queen had magic powers and owned a
wondrous mirror that spoke. Every day she stood
before it and asked:

Magic mirror on the wall,
Who is the fairest one of all?

And every day the mirror answered:

You are the fairest of all, O Queen,
The fairest our eyes have ever seen.

As time passed, Snow White grew more and more beautiful—and the Queen grew more and more envious. So she forced the Princess to dress in rags and work in the kitchen from dawn to dusk.

Despite all the hard work, Snow White stayed sweet, gentle, and cheerful.

Day after day she washed and swept and scrubbed. And day after day she dreamed of a handsome Prince who would come and carry her off to his castle.

One day when the Queen spoke to her mirror, it
replied with the words she had been dreading:

Fair is thy beauty, Majesty,
But hold—a lovely maid I see,
One who is more fair than thee.
Lips red as a rose, hair black as ebony,
   skin white as snow…

"Snow White?" shrieked the angry Queen. "She
must be destroyed!"

The Queen sent for her huntsman.

"Take Snow White deep into the forest," she said, "and there, my faithful one, you will kill her."

The unhappy man begged the Queen to be merciful, but she would not be persuaded. "Remember my magic powers," she warned. "Obey me, or you and your family will suffer!"

The next day Snow White, never suspecting that
she was in danger, went off with the huntsman.

When they were deep in the woods, the huntsman
drew his knife. Then, suddenly, he fell to his knees.

"I can't kill you," he sobbed. "Forgive me, sweet
Princess. It was the Queen who ordered this wicked
deed."

"The Queen?" gasped Snow White.

"She's mad with jealousy," said the huntsman. "She'll stop at nothing to destroy you. Quick—run away and don't come back. I'll think of something to tell the Queen. Now, go! Run! Save yourself!"

Frightened, Snow White fled through the woods. Tangled branches tore at her clothes. Sharp twigs scratched her arms and legs. Strange eyes stared from the shadows. Danger lurked everywhere.

Snow White ran on and on. At last she fell wearily to the ground and began to weep.

The gentle animals of the forest gathered around and tried to comfort her. Chirping and chattering, they led her to a tiny cottage.

"Oh," said Snow White, "how sweet! It's just like a doll's house."

But inside, the tiny furniture was all dusty, and the sink was filled with dirty dishes.

"Let's tidy everything up," said Snow White. "Maybe the children who live here will let me stay and take care of them."

The animals all helped, and soon the place was spick-and-span.

Meanwhile, the Seven Dwarfs who lived in the cottage were starting home from the mine where they worked. On their way they sang:

Heigh-ho, Heigh-ho,
It's home from work we go...

The Dwarfs were amazed to find their house so
neat and clean. They were even more amazed when
they tiptoed upstairs and saw Snow White!

Snow White woke up with a start. "Why, you're
not children," she said when she saw the Dwarfs.
"You're little men!"

The Dwarfs gathered around her.

"I read your names on the beds," said Snow
White. "Let me guess who you are. You must be
Doc. And you must be Bashful. Then there's Sneezy,
and Sleepy, and Happy, and Dopey...and *you* must
be Grumpy!"

When Snow White told the Dwarfs of the Queen's plan to kill her, they decided that she should stay with them.

"We're askin' for trouble," huffed Grumpy.

"But we *can't* let her be caught by that kwicked ween—I mean, wicked Queen!" said Doc. The others all agreed.

That night, after supper, Snow White and the Dwarfs
danced and made merry music. Bashful played the concertina.
Happy tapped the drums. Sleepy tooted the horn. Grumpy
pumped the organ. Doc and Sneezy played stringed instruments.
Dopey didn't know how to sing or play a tune, but he
was very good at wiggling his ears!

Snow White loved her new friends. And she felt safe at last.

But the Queen had learned from her mirror that Snow White was still alive. "This time," she hissed, "I'll finish her myself!"

With a magic spell, she turned herself into an old peddler woman. She filled a basket with apples, putting a poisoned apple on top. "One bite," she cackled, "and Snow White will sleep forever. Then *I* will be the fairest in the land!"

Next morning, before the Dwarfs left for the mine, they warned Snow White to be on her guard.

"Beware of strangers," said Doc.

"Right," said Grumpy. "Don't let nobody or nothin' in the house."

"Oh, Grumpy," said Snow White, "you *do* care! I'll be careful, I promise." She kissed him and the others good-by, and the Dwarfs went cheerfully off to work.

A few minutes later, the Queen came to the
kitchen window.

"Baking pies, dearie?" she asked. "It's *apple* pies
the men love. Here, taste one of these." She held the
poisoned apple out to Snow White.

Snow White remembered the Dwarfs' warning.
"But what harm can a poor old woman do?" she
thought. "And that apple does look delicious."

She bit the poisoned apple. Then, with a sigh, she
fell to the floor.

Alerted by the birds and animals that something was wrong, the Dwarfs raced back to the cottage. They saw the Queen sneaking off, and they ran after her.

As storm clouds gathered and rain began to fall, the Dwarfs chased the Queen up a high, rocky mountain. Up, up they went, to the very top.

CRACK! There was a flash of lightning, and the evil Queen fell to her doom below.

But the Dwarfs seemed to be too late to help Snow White. They lifted her lifeless body from the floor of their cottage. She was so beautiful, however, that the Dwarfs could not bear to part with her. They built her a coffin of glass and gold, and day and night they kept watch over their beloved Princess.

One day a handsome Prince came riding through
the forest. As soon as he saw Snow White, he fell in
love with her. Kneeling by her coffin, he could not
resist kissing her.

Snow White sat up, blinked her eyes, and smiled.
Snow White wasn't dead after all. The Prince's kiss
had broken the Queen's evil spell!

As the Dwarfs danced with joy, the Prince carried
Snow White off to his castle, where they lived
happily ever after.